We're Having a
SUPER
BABY

Written by Abie Longstaff
Illustrated by Jane Massey

SCHOLASTIC

"Guess what?" said Daddy.
"You're going to be a big brother," said Mummy.

I was SO excited!

I spent ages getting
everything ready.

At long last, one snowy day, my baby sister came home.

At first she didn't do much.

Mummy said she couldn't fly to space yet.

Daddy said she wasn't ready to sail the seven seas.

But I knew she was going to be special.
I just had to wait.

So I waited...

...and I waited...

...and I waited...

...until the day when I discovered
something really special...

My sister has super powers!

She can speed across the floor so
fast using her Mighty Tummy Crawl.

Everyone is amazed how quickly she can empty the cupboard...

...or pull down all the books from the bookshelf to make a Super Mess.

Every day she does her Amazing Exercises:

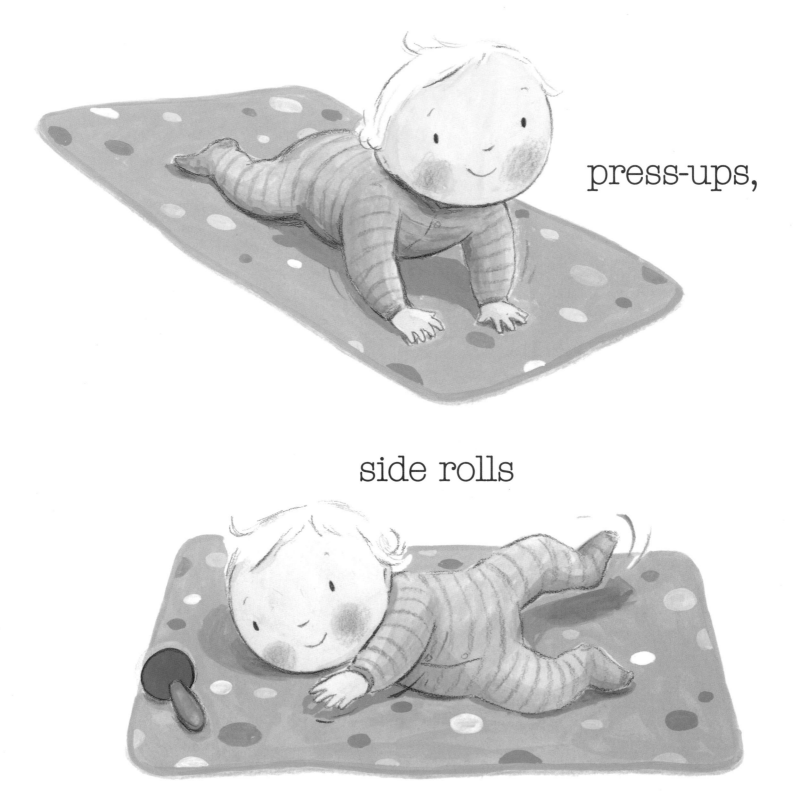

press-ups,

side rolls

and kung fu.

She is so strong that when she
doesn't like her dinner...

...we really know about it.

Sometimes, my sister and
I are superheroes together.

I wear my
special outfit,

and she wears her Super Suit.

We keep a lookout for anyone in need.

If she sees someone in trouble,
my sister does her Power Yell and
wiggles her toes to tell me what to do...

...so we save the day.

When it's too wet to go to the park,
we build ourselves a Top-Secret Den.

And we use our
Super Shout to yell,
"Rain, *rain*
GO AWAY!"

My sister even has a secret weapon to
scare off all enemies:

The power of Stinky Nappies!

She is so super that...

there is only one thing that can stop her...

...Sleep.

But not for long!
So watch out, baddies, because...

...Here comes
Super
Baby!